J. T. Vegiard

The Dutch Recruit

The blue and gray

J. T. Vegiard

The Dutch Recruit
The blue and gray

ISBN/EAN: 9783337302771

Printed in Europe, USA, Canada, Australia, Japan

Cover: Foto ©Andreas Hilbeck / pixelio.de

More available books at **www.hansebooks.com**

—— OR, ——

THE BLUE AND GRAY.

AN ORIGINAL ALLEGORICAL DRAMA OF THE CIVIL WAR OF 1861--66.

IN FIVE ACTS,

J. RD.

—— ——

A DESCRIPTION OF TH OF THE CHARACTERS—
ENTRANCES AND POSITIONS OF THE
PERFORMERS D THE WHOLE
OF SS.

DEDICAT ANS.”

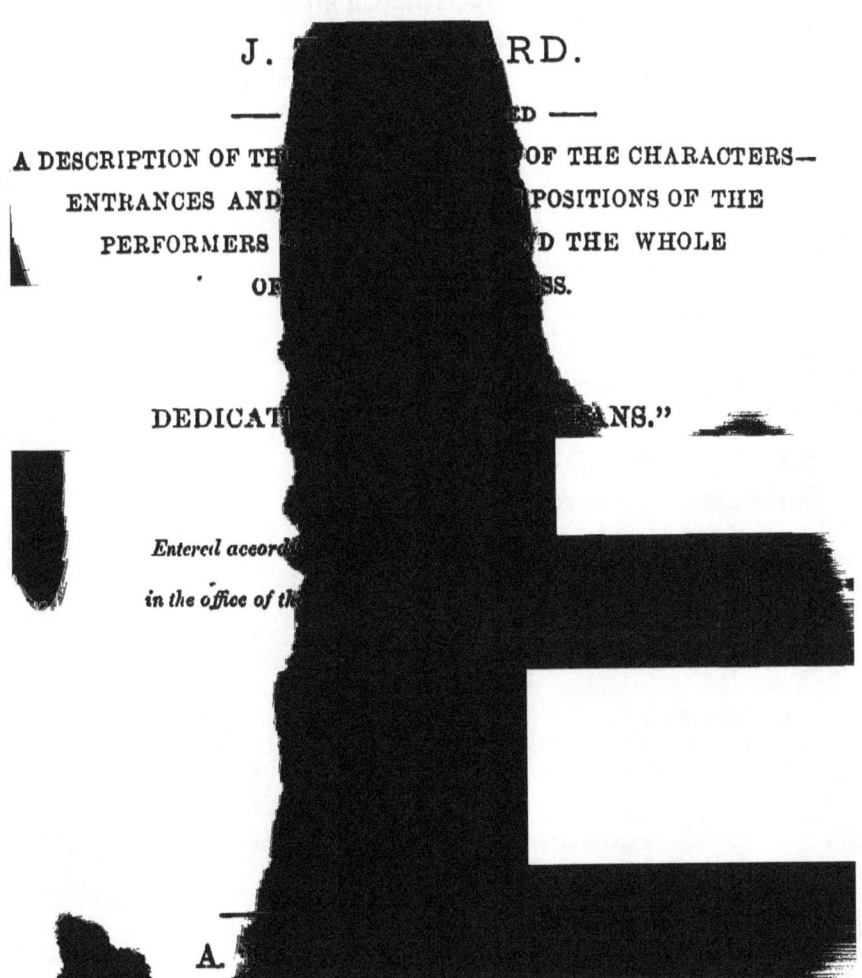

Entered accord

in the office of th

A.

THE DUTCH RECRUIT, OR THE BLUE AND GRAY.

───o───

CHARACTERS.

DEITRICH VONDERSPECK   (The Dutch Recruit)
COL. SL. LEON   (a loyal Southerner)
HARRY PEARSON   (a Union Spy)
FRANK DUNCAN   (The Guerrilla Chieftain)
JOHN HARKER (St. Leon's Overseer, afterwards a Guerrilla)
CHARLES WHITE   (Harry's friend, a Union Scout)
TEDDY O'CONNOR   (a son of the Old Sod)
GENERAL   (Commanding U. S Forces)
COL. FRANKLIN   (of the U. S. Army)
UNCLE NED   (an Octogenarian)
GENERAL   (Commanding C. S. Forces)
SAM   (one of the Bones of Contention)
ALEX. BURT   (A Lieutenant of Guerrillas)
PRISONER   (at Belle Isle)
MAUDE ST. LEON   (a loyal lady, daughter of St. Leon)
MRS. ST. LEON   (Wife of the Colonel)
GODDESS OF LIBERTY

Officers U. S. A.   Officers C. S. A.   Citizens, Soldiers, Bushwhackers, Prisoners, etc., etc.

───o───

STAGE DIRECTIONS.

R., means Right; L., Left; R. H., Right Hand; L. H., Left Hand; C., Centre; S. E.; [2d E.,] Second Entrance; U. E., Upper Entrance; M. D., Middle Door; F., the Flat. D. F., Door in Flat; R. C., Right of Centre; L. C., Left of Centre.

R.   R. C.   C.   L. C.   L.

*** The reader is supposed to be upon the stage facing the audience.

───

Parties who desire to produce this play, are at liberty to do so free of all royalty.   *The Publisher.*

COSTUMES.

COL. ST. LEON. Plain gray, or light suit, broad hat, cane.

HARRY PEARSON. *Act 1, Scene 1*—Riding suit, light. *Scene 3*—Hunting suit. *Act 2*—Dark suit, cape. *Act 4, Scene 3*—Torn shirt and pants, old shoes. *Scene 4 and 5*—Gray jacket, slouch hat. *Act 5*—Same as Act 2, with head bandaged.

FRANK DUNCAN. Gray officer's suit, sword, etc.

JOHN HARKER. *Act 1, Scene 1*—Light suit, slouch hat, broad white collar and cuffs, heavy whip. *Scene 2*—Gray officer's suit, sword, etc.

DEITRICH. *Act 1*—Common overalls. *Act 2*—Old Union uniform, large front piece on cap, gun. *Act 4*—Calico dress, dutch bonnet. *Act 5*—Same as Act 2.

CHARLES WHITE. Hunting suit. *Act 4, Scene 3-4*—White wig and whiskers, long coat, broad hat and cane.

TEDDY. *Act 1*—Knee pants, overshirt, old silk hat. *Acts 2, 4, and 5*—Gray jacket, slouch hat, gun.

ALEX. BURT. *Act 1*—Rough citizen's dress. *Acts 2, 4, and 5*—Officers gray suit, sword, etc.

GENERAL U. S. A. Heavy overcoat, revolver, side arms.

COL. FRANKLIN. Heavy overcoat, revolver, side arms.

GENERAL C. S. A. Full dress Confederate gray, sword etc.

UNCLE NED. *Act 1*—Short pants, shoes and stockings, checkered shirt, sleeves rolled up, curled white wig. *Act 2*—Long coat, old white silk hat.

SAM. *Act 1*—Livery, top boots, etc.

PRISONERS. Old blue uniforms.

SOLDIERS U. S. A. Blue blouses, fatigue caps, light blue pants.

SOLDIERS C. S. A. and GUERRILLAS. Gray suits, slouch hats.

MAUDE ST. LEON. *Act 1, Scene 1*—Riding habit, whip. *Scene 5-6*—Light house dress. *Act 4*—Dark dress, cloak or shawl, hat. *Act 5*—Dark dress.

MRS. ST. LEON. House dress for old lady, spectacles. *Acts 4-5*—Dark dress, cloak or shawl, hat.

GODDESS OF LIBERTY. Full Goddess dress.

SCENE PLOT.

———o———

ACT I.

Scene 1—Garden or landscape in 4th grooves.
Scene 2—Landscape or street in 1st grooves.
Scene 3—Plain room or kitchen in 3d grooves.
Scene 4—Landscape or street in 1st grooves.
Scene 5—Parlor in 2d grooves.
Scene 6—Same as scene 1st.

ACT II.

Scene 1—Log house or kitchen in 4th grooves.
Scene 2—Landscape in 2d grooves.
Scene 3—Wood in 1st grooves.
Scene 4—Log house or kitchen in 4th—Same as
  scene 1st.

ACT III.

Scene 1—Landscape, full depth of **Stage** for drill.

ACT IV.

Scene 1—Garden or landscape in 4th grooves, same
  as scene 1st, act 1st.
Scene 2—Landscape in 1st grooves.
Scene 3—Stockade in 3d grooves.
Scene 4—Landscape in 1st grooves.
Scene 5—Rocky Pass in 4th grooves.

ACT V.

Scene 1—Dark wood or rocky pass in 4th grooves.
Scene 2—Wood in 2d grooves,
Scene 3—Same as scene 1st.

THE DUTCH RECRUIT;
OR, THE BLUE AND GRAY.

─────o─────

ACT 1.

SCENE 1—Garden or Landscape in 4; Set house L. 3
E.; *set fence* L. *to* R.; *gate open* C., *bench lying* R.; *Negroes discovered dancing. At conclusion* UNCLE NED
enters R. 1 E. *with garden rake.*

Uncle Ned. Git out dar, you good-for-nuffin niggahs;
Clar de grounds! (*all scatter and exit* R. *and* L., *appearing at intervals from behind wings*) What de goodness
you 'spose dis niggah's gwine to do? Clar de lawn for you
common niggahs to dance on? Clar out dar, I say! (*leans
on rake*) I golly, dem niggahs 'spose dat I have nuffin' at
all to do but clean up after dem. 'Taint no use talking, I'm
done wid dem. De fust time I ketch um on dis lawn I
scrunch dem like a bed bug, suah! (*Negroes steal out and
commence dancing.* NED *chases them* R. *and* L.) Clar dar,
you niggahs! Clar dar, I say!

Enter, HARKER L. 1 E., *with whip.*

Harker. Get to your work, you black rascals, or I'll
skin every one of you. And you, Ned, go into the house,
the cook may have errands for you to do at the village.
Uncle Ned. (*bowing*) All right, Massa Harker, and if
I ketch any of dem common niggahs 'round here, I'll scrunch
'em suah.
Har. Don't stand around here talking, but go at once.
(*exit* NED, L. U. E.) I understand Frank Duncan has returned to the village — if he has, then I can see him personally and accept his proposition. (*takes letter from his pocket and reads*) "HARKER, I hold in my possession a Lieutenancy in the Confederate Army; join me and the position is
yours. I will be in the village with my company in a few
days. If you can enlist any men, do so, and meet me at
Munson's store. Yours, FRANK DUNCAN." Ah, here comes
the Colonel.

Enter, COLONEL ST. LEON, L.

Col St L. Well, Harker, how are the farm hands doing this morning?   (*Crosses to* R., HARKER *to* L.

Har. I keep them pretty busy now, Colonel: by the by, is there any news stirring?

Col St L. War, war, nothing but war. Ah! what is this? (*reads from newspaper*) "Two men belonging to a notorious band of bushwhackers, commanded by that master cut-throat, Frank Duncan, were hung at Montford last Tuesday." So ho! Frank Duncan, instead of entering the Confederate service proper, which would have been bad enough, has turned Guerrilla. And that is the man who wanted my daughter to become his wife. The infernal villain!

Har. (*aside*) I must get away from here. (*looking* R. *aloud*) Excuse me Colonel, but there are some of those lazy rascals dodging behind the stables. (*snapping whip*) Get to your work, you infernal niggers, get to your work!   (*exit* R. 2 E.

Enter, UNCLE NED L. 1 E.

Uncle Ned. Oh, Massa Kurnel, I saw dat Massa Duncan down to de village, dressed up in nice grey clothes wid stars and gold all ober him, and he had such a big cheese knife; golly!

Col St L. Frank Duncan in town; I fear his presence means no good to the Union men of this vicinity. Thus far we have not been molested; but his presence bodes evil.

Uncle Ned. I golly, Massa Kurnel, here comes de debbil hisself!   (UNCLE NED *up stage*

Enter, FRANK DUNCAN L. 1 E.

Frank Duncan. Ah, St. Leon, how are you to-day. Won't shake hands? No. Well, suit yourself. (*aside*) By and by, St. Leon, you will sing another tune.

Col St L. I am sorry I can't tender you the honors of my house; but to what purpose shall I attribute the honor of this unexpected visit, Mr. Duncan?

Frank D. (*aside*) He used to call me his boy Frank. (*aloud*) Colonel, you are not a stranger to the fact that before I entered the Confederate service I loved your daughter, and sought her hand from you honorably; you refused to consent to my addresses. Sir, that love has grown stronger. I now ask you to reconsider the decision you made at my last visit.

Col St L. The decision I then made remains irrevocable. I would never consent that a daughter of mine should marry a man who has basely deserted his country's flag in its hour of danger. This is not only my decision, but my daughter would scorn to wed a man who cannot even boast of being an honorable rebel.

Frank D. (*quickly*) Whe dares to say I am not a true and honorable soldier.

Col St L. This will explain all. (*reads from newspaper*) "Two men belonging to a notorious band of bushwhackers, commanded by that master cut-throat, Frank Duncan, were hung at Montford last Tuesday."

Frank D. (*aside*) Curse those fools, they have betrayed my secret! Nothing but a bold face will serve me now, (*aloud*) I assure you Colonel, it is all a mistake.

Col St L. It is not a mistake: (*looks* R.) but here comes my daughter Maude, she shall give the final decision.

Enter, MAUDE ST LEON, R. 2 E. *followed by* SAM.

Maude. Father, I had such a splendid ride; Gipsey took me across the brook by the old mill, thence over the hedge and—

Col St L. You do not notice we have company, Maude.

Maude. I was not aware. Why, Mr. Duncan!

Frank D. Mr. Duncan again. (*aloud*) Miss Maude I had hoped for a better reception after so prolonged an absence.

Col St L. My child, to save further words, and you and Mr. Duncan from any embarrassment, I will at once state the object of his visit. He wishes me to withdraw my former decision in reference to his suit, and I have, thus far, as I always wish to consult my child's happiness—everything is left in your hands, Are you willing to marry Frank Duncan?

Maude. Father, your decision was mine. Mr. Duncan, I cannot marry a man, however much I might love him, who would raise his hand in opposition to his country's flag.

Col St L. My own noble girl! Spoken like a St. Leon.

Frank D. Maude, one word.

Maude. Mr. Duncan, it is needless to prolong this interview, and as you have some business of a private nature to transact with father I may be in the way. Good morning, sir. Follow me, Sam. *(they exit* L.

Frank D. *(aside)* Yes, we may have some business of a private nature to transact, but not at present. *(aloud)* Sir, I can but regret the decision of yourself and daughter, but I shall hope that time may change your views.

Col St L. Mr. Duncan, you have heard my decision, which, as I have said before, is irrevocable.

Frank D. Hark you, St, Leon, I have made a decision as irrevocable as yours. Your daughter shall be my wife, though I wade through oceans of blood to obtain her, and if it must be, every house in the township shall be a beacon light to guide me in my purpose.

Col St L. Leave my plantation instantly, sir! You dare to threaten a St. Leon! Leave, sir, or I will order the negroes to assist you.

Frank D. No need of such needless trouble, Colonel St. Leon, I will take my leave, *(aside)* but will soon return.

(exit L. 1 E.

Uncle Ned. Massa Kurnel, shan't I bounce him?

Col St L. The infernal scoundrel! To threaten my name with such a dishonor. By jove, I'm sorry I didn't chastise him before he left.

Uncle Ned. Only say de word, Massa Kurnel, and I'll hab de boys ketch him and chuck him in de hoss-pond, and if he says a word I'll scrunch him like a bed-bug, suah.

Col St L. Never mind this time, Ned.

Enter, MRS. ST. LEON, *and* MAUDE *from house* L.

Mrs St Leon. Colonel, what was the meaning of that loud talking we just heard?

Col St L. That insolent traitor, Frank Duncan has been here, and threatened that if I did not—but pshaw, no matter. Is dinner nearly ready?

Maude. Yes, father, dinner is ready; but we were waiting for Harry, he has not yet returned from his ride.

Harry. *(outside)* Here, Sam, tell Julius to stable my horse.

Enter, HARRY PEARSON L. 2 E.

Harry Pearson. Ah, aunt, waiting dinner for me, sorry to have kept you. Maude, how do you like your new horse, Gipsey?

Maude. Harry, he is a perfect beauty, and as easy under the saddle as one could wish. You have my thanks for the present; but who do you think has been here this morning?

Harry. I am in the dark, who was it?

Maude. Frank Duncan.

Harry. That accounts for the town being full of cut-throats.

Col St L. I have no doubt they belong to his gang. I fear for the Union men of this vicinity.

Mrs St L. Oh, Colonel, I fear the worst. What will become of us all?

Harry. Become of us? Thank God there are loyal hearts among us who will never shrink from any peril for their country's sake.

Maude. I am sure, Harry, that you will do your best to protect us from this band of assassins.

Enter, SAM, L.

Sam. Massa Kurnel, de dinner am done spoiling.

Col St L. Come, mother, Maude, Harry, let us to our dinner at once. (*they exit* L.

Uncle Ned. I golly, Sam, dar's gwine to be a muss suah.

Sam. Gorry mitey, Uncle, is dat so?

Uncle Ned. Dat's what's de matter. But Sam are you gwine to fite?

Sam. Me fite? Wha' for?

Uncle Ned. For your massa, missus, and de old plantation.

Sam. Look heah, Uncle, you've seen two dogs fitin' ober a bone?

Uncle Ned. Yes.

Sam. Dat's de Norf an' Souf fitin' ober us. Now Uncle, did you eber see de bone fite? But come 'long to de kitchen.

Uncle Ned. Hold on, Sam, de ole man's got de rumatics—hold on—hold on! (*exeunt* L. U. E.

SCENE II—Landscape.

Enter, FRANK DUNCAN, R. 1 E.

Frank D. So, the doors of the St. Leon mansion are closed against me; little did I think a few hours ago that I should be an outcast from the family where I have always, even from childhood, been received as a friend. My hopes of winning Maude are forever blasted. I will try to forget her. I cannot, her image is firmly implanted in the inmost recesses of my heart. Shall I tamely give her up while my rival, Pearson, curses on him, carries off the prize? No! by all the powers of heaven and earth, she shall be mine!

Enter, HARKER R. 1 E.

So, Harker, you received the letter I sent you last week?

Har. Yes, Frank, and acting upon your warrant contained therein, I procured this uniform and several men for your band.

Frank D. Well done, Harker. We will visit the men at once, and our first job will be to ransack and burn the St. Leon mansion, then off to our rendezvous before any of those cursed Yankee scouts happen around this vicinity.

Har. I am with you in any scheme against that old aristocrat.

Frank D. Why, what have you against St. Leon?

Har. (*bitterly*) Enough! Has he not treated me more like a servant than as an equal, and when I have punished any of his niggers hasn't he interfered, while his family act as if I was unfit to sit in their presence. I hate them all.

Frank D. Well, we will make them suffer for our many wrongs. You take some of these notices I have prepared, and place them in conspicuous places. Come along with me as far as the Cross Roads and we will perfect our plans, I will then meet you at Munson's shortly. (*exeunt* L. 1 E.

Enter, UNCLE NED R. 1 E.

Uncle Ned. Dar he goes along wid Massa Harker, plottin' 'gainst my ole Massa Kurnel. Well, de ole man must stir his bones and go to de house. Dese yere are troublesome times and I fear de colored people of de lan' will hab to stand de brunt. Well, don't stand yere makin' an ole fool ob yerself, but git along. (*exit* L. 1 E.

SCENE III--Plain chamber or kitchen in 3d grooves.
Bar L. *Tables and chairs* R. *and* L. ALEX BURT *and*
CITIZENS *standing near bar.* TEDDY *and* DEITRICH R.
playing cards.

Burt. Step up, boys, and have a drink with me.
(CITIZENS *go to the bar*
Teddy. Mr. Deitrich, it's a taking of my thrick ye are.
Hand thim cards back, ye spalpeen.
Deitrich. Vell I link so neider, ven I puts a veller mit
his two heats to both ends down you dook him to dot side,
und you put a veller mit his dwo heats to both ends down,
I dook him, dot is goot.
Ted. Arrah now, sure the thrick is mine whin yees
didn't thrump nor follow suit.
Deitrich. Nein—nein I knows me out notting und I
gares notting apout your drumps und shoots. Vot I vant
vonce is mein rights—you dake him ouf von drick und I
dakes him ouf von drick, dot is goot, den dot vas my durn,
but you dalks apout your drumps und shoots und dakes all
der dricks und I nix-for-stay, und gits mat of meinselfund
don'd plays mit a veller vot vants to sheat me. (*down stage* R.
Ted. (*down stage* L.) Say hare, you stuttering dutch
lunatic, do yese mane to say that Teddy O'Connor was a
chate? Bad cess to yese for a haythen as doesn't know wan
card from anither. (BURT *crosses stage*
Burt. Hello! What's all this disputing about, I'd like
to know?
Deitrich. I knows not dis veller pefore, und I tinks he
vas a lunadic asylum mit der straight jacket drown in, und
I finds him to been von sheat dot vants all der gards for
himself, und dot's gusht vot I vants meinself.
Ted. Did yese iver see such a fool at all, Alex? He
thinks we play cards this way—I puts down a card and he
takes it, thin he puts down a card and thin I takes it; wan
card is as good as anither to him, and the jack takes thim all.
Deitrich. Nein—nein, dot is not so, it's petter I vas a
fool ain't it? I vants me not all der gards, I gusht vants
mine chare.
Burt. Well, haven't you got your chair?
(*points to chair*

Deitrich. Dundervedder! I don'd mean mine chare dot
I sets mineself down on—I mean mine chare ouf der gards.
I gusht got ein—swi—dry—dimes, (*counting fingers*) und
he has more dimes as me.

Burt. Oh, I see, you want his dimes—his money. If I
was Teddy I wouldn't give you a picayune.

Deitrich. I tinks you bese dhrunk like der tuyval, you
gits every ting by der tail out. I tole you again apout dot.
Ve plays gards, you knows dot—he dakes him ouf von drick
und I dakes him ouf von drick, den dot vas mine turn, but
he no lets me dake ouf his drick, but he dakes mine und I
never sees like dot now.

Burt. Ah, yes, I see, he euchered you, didn't he?

Deitrich. Nein, he no shucker me, he sheats me—und
dalks apout his drumps und shoots—but ouf he says dot
more as droo hours longer I gife mineself a plack eyes.

Ted. Be aff wid ye, be aff. I wants yees to remimber
that I have desinded from the Irish Kings. Me ansister,
Roderick O'Connor, was Prince of Connaught, and whin
ould Pimbroke was a ravigin' Ireland, he was elected King
sure; he fit—till he got licked and thin he gave up, and av
yese give me any more of yer blarney I'll put a hid on yese.

Deitrich. So help me gracious, I can't stand dot more as
doo hours longer!

TEDDY *and* DEITRICK *rush at each other.* BURT *and* CITI-
ZENS *take* TEDDY L. *to bar.*

Deitrich. Dree or four vellers hold him, I holds mineself.

Enter, HARKER *and* SERGEANT C. S. A.

Har. What do you mean by all this noise?

Deitrich. Dot's none ouf mine bisness.

Har. Here, Sergeant, stick that bill up there.
  (*all gather raound to see what it is,* HARKER *at bar.*
Ted. (*spells the words out slowly*) All a-b-l-e, all able,
b-o-d-i-e-d, all able bodied min—

Dietrich. (*throwing* TEDDY L.) Sthand pack, I reads
mineself ouf dot. (*pushing* CITIZENS R. *and* L.) Sthand pack!
(*to* SERGEANT *who stands* R., *should be a tall man*) Sthand
pack! (SERGEANT *does not move*—DEITRICH *goes to push
him, looks up*) You needn't sthir, sthand right there.

(gets up in a chair and reads) ``All aple podied men pe-
tween der ages ouf swantiz und fiftiz are—

Ted. Are— *(drawing it out*

Deitrich. Are—

Ted. Are—

Deitrich. Are—

Ted. Are—

Deitrich. Shut up, Irishmans, you can't read dot I
don'd can tell what dot pig word he vas. Mr. Burt, you
reads dot ouf me. *(down* R.) You can't reads?

Ted. You old odmahaun!

Burt. *(reads)* "All able bodied men between the ages
of twenty and fifty are earnestly called upon to join the
Southern Army. Rally to the call of your countrymen
in the field. One united effort and those Northern hirelings
will be driven from our Sunny South."

Har. Come, boys, what will you have to drink? 1 am
as dry as a fish out of water.

(all go to the bar, and call for drinks

Deitrich. I dook a glass ouf peer mit you.

(goes to bar L., HAUKER *next, then* TEDDY.

Ted. Rather than see yese drink alone, I'll take Irish
whisky straight av yese have it.

Har. All right, my man, take something. *(they drink
then come down stage)* You will make a good soldier; what
do you say, don't you want to join the Southern Army?

Ted. Sure and I'll do that same thing if yese give me
good pay and plinty of foightin'.

Har. We can promise you both, but have another
drink. *(all go to bar*

Enter, FRANK DUNCAN, L. 1 E.

Deitrich. I dook some more peer.

Frank D. Rejected by Maude, who once professed to
love me. The one for whom I would sacrifice life itself,
with all its pleasures. Driven from the plantation by that
old dotard, St. Leon. Curse them, but they will pay dearly for it yet.

Har. Have something, Captain?

Frank D. *(to bar)* Yes, give me brandy. I feel as if
I could drink an ocean-dry, *(filling glass drinks)* there,

I feel better now. I was a little out of sorts just now. Deitrich, give us a song!

All. A song—a song!

Deitrich. Vell, I got a horse in mine dhroat und a colt in mine hed put I sing von leedle songs.

* *Song introduced—"Dere vas a Leedle Deitcher Maid."*

Frank D. Any more men secured, Harker?

Har. I just came in, but Burt has been busy with them.

Burt. They will all go. What do you say my brave fellows?

All. Y-es—yes!

Frank D. Thank you boys, and I'll give each of you a chance to make a fortune.

Burt. Hurrah for the Captain.

All. Hurrah! Hurrah! Hurrah!

Enter, HARRY *and* WHITE L. 1 E.

Frank D. Ah, how are you boys, none in uniform! How is this Pearson? I thought you would be one of the first to rush to the aid of the unhappy South.

Harry. I am wanted at home to attend to my old uncle, aunt and cousin, in fact I am a stay-at-home character.

Frank D. In place of hiding under petticoats, own up that you have no heart in the Southern cause.

Harry. Have it your own way, anything to avoid unpleasant argument.

Frank D. Here, Munson, set up the drinks. Come boys, have something. (BARTENDER *sets glasses on stand* C.

Deitrich. I dook a glass ouf peer mit you. (*pushing* TEDDY *back*) You don'd got none, Irisher, I got a pig drink mineself.

TEDDY *shakes fist—all take up glasses but* BURT, *just as* DEITRICH *reaches for his glass* BURT *picks it up,* DEITRICH *gets mad*—TEDDY *laughs.*

Frank D. Here's to the health of Jefferson Davis and the Southern Confederacy. Come, Pearson and White, show your colors, don't be afraid.

Harry. (*they put down glasses*) Afraid! No sir. I am not afraid to say that I despise and detest you and your

* **Can be had of Mr. Ames. Price 30 cents.**

whole pack of cut-throats just as much as I despise your President, and your would-be Confederacy. I have thus far been neutral, but my heart and sympathies are with the Union now and forever. (DEITRICH *and* TEDDY *pick up glasses*

White. Bravo! Harry, I am with you.

Deitrich. I don'd drink 'em ouf dot doast—but I drinks ouf dis—Ein flag, ein gountry—swi lager. (*drinks*

Ted. I drinks 'em both, divil a wan I cares as long as I gets me foightin'. (*drinks*

Frank D. So, Harry Pearson, you follow in the footsteps of your uncle, and take issue with the enemies of the South. Now mark me, I am vested with power from my government to force such as you into our army, and you need not fear but I shall use it.

Harry. Frank Duncan, you have had your say, now I will have mine. I defy you or any force you can bring to force me to raise a hand against the glorious old Stars and Stripes.

Frank D. You have till dark to make up your minds, then if you are not ready to go willingly force shall be used.

Harry. Come, White, let us finish our hunt, after to-day we shall have larger game. (*they exit* L.

Deitrich. (*rushes up to* FRANK DUNCAN) I gone mineself out und ven ve meets look— (*goes* L. 1 E., TEDDY *kicks at him and falls over*—FRANK DUNCAN *starts toward Deitrich, who exits* L.

Frank D. Men, to the camp. Harker, take charge till I arrive. (*all exit* L. 1 E.) Curse the luck, it has been disappointment after disappointment to-day, but I will yet humble the pride of the St. Leons. First to force that young braggart into our army, and if he refuses to go, shoot him down like a dog. (*exit* L. 1 E.

SCENE IV—Landscape—Lights half down.

Enter, HARRY, WHITE *and* DEITRICH R. 1 E.

Harry. Well here it is evening, and none of us have decided to join the Southern army. I suppose we shall be severely punished for our temerity.

White. I shall not allow the fear of Frank Duncan's wrath to spoil my appetite, and as it is growing late I will bid you good evening; come Deitrich. (*exit* L. 1 E.

Deitrich. Vell, I got some abbedite doo und I eat dot supper gust so quick as I get him.

Harry. (*calls*) White, remember the signal!

White. (*outside*) All right—'two shots.'

Deitrich. All richt, dwo shoots.   (*exit* L. 1 E.

Harry. I have had strange forebodings of evil all day upon my mind. At every flash of our guns Uncle and Frank Duncan would rise before me. What can it mean? But I must shake off these feelings of depression and consider what course to pursue. It will be unsafe for me to remain around here while Frank Duncan and his men are in such close proximity, and I do not relish going into the army either as an officer or private. What else can I do? I have it! I know every part of this State thoroughly and I will tender my services to the Union General to act as a spy. I will first consult with my Uucle and if he is willing go at once.   (*exit* L. 1 E.

SCENE V—*Parlor in* 2. *Set window* R.

Enter, MRS. ST. LEON *and* MAUDE R. 1 E.

Maude. I wonder what keeps Harry, he is not usually detained so long while hunting. (*going to window*) I hope nothing has happened.

Mrs St L. Do not be impatient child, Harry will, no doubt, be here soon.

Enter, COL. ST. LEON, C. D.

Maude. Father, I believe Harry wishes to join the Union army, he has spoken to me several times about it of late, but he thought his first duty was with you and mother.

Enter, HARRY, C.

Col St L. If it is his wish, I shall make no opposition.

Harry. Thank you, uncle for those cheering words. Frank Duncan and I had a few sharp words at Munson's store to-day, which resulted in my openly avowing my principles, and he swears that he will either force me into his cut-throat band or shoot me down like a dog.

Col St L. The infernal scoundrel!

Harry. Uncle, I feel that the time has now arrived for me to join the Union army, and do my share toward putting down this Rebellion.

Col St L.   Yes, Harry, your duty points that way; take the best horse in the stable, make your way to the Union camp, and tell the General that old Col. St. Leon has sent you to take his place in the conflict.

Maude.   Why, Harry, surely you are not going so soon?

Harry.   The sooner the better, Maude, once in the Union lines I can meet Frank Duncan face to face.   I with the Blue he with the Gray.

Mrs St L.   Harry, 'tis hard to bid you leave us, but far be it from me to keep you even one moment from your duty.

Maude.   My dear cousin, you have our prayers for your success.

Harry.   Thank you all for your kind wishes, but I do not go alone.   (*fires two shots out window*)   Do not be alarmed, 'tis but a signal to call my friends.

Enter, DEITRICH, *quickly* C.

Deitrich.   Misder Harry, I comes ouf mineself down as I vants to sprecken doo dimes mit Uncle der Kurnel.

Col St L.   Well, Deitrich, what can I do for you?

Deitrich.   I tinks dot I gots a situation from der army out, und I wish you would geep ouf dot money dot you owes your seef ouf me, und ouf I gots kilt—(*aside*)—der deuce, suppose I gets kilt!   (*aloud*)   Vell, ouf I vas got kilt gif it to dem boorhouses.   (*crosses to* R.

Col St L.   I will attend to your bequest.

Harry.   We are not going alone, Deitrich, for here comes company.

Deitrich.   Ish dot so?

Enter, WHITE, C.

White.   I heard the signal and hastened here at once. What has happened?

Harry.   Nothing of importance, but I have decided to make my way to the Union camp, and wishing company, I called you here.   Will you both join me, as I go for one?

White.   Count me as two.

Deterich.   So I dree dimes.   (*crosses* L.

                    (MRS. ST. LEON *goes to the window*

Harry.   Thank you friends for your decision, but we must make arrangements for our immediate departure.

Mrs St L.   Harry, there must be something unusual going on at Munson's store, as a large crowd has gathered
there.

Enter, MAUDE, C.

Maude.   Fly, Harry!   Fly at once, Frank Duncan is
coming to force you to join his band.

Harry.   Never fear, Maude, he shall not find me unpre-
pared.   (*exit, returns immediately with rifle which he places near window*)   There is one good shot at least.

Maude.   Oh, Harry, fly for my sake, do not, I pray you,
tarry here.   I hear them even now.

Col St L.   Resistance is useless to such numbers, there-
fore, do not turn our home into a scene of desolation and
blood-shed, but fly at once. (*exit* WHITE *and* DEITRICH, C.

Harry.   Uncle, though I detest a skulker and a coward,
you shall be obeyed.   Farewell, Uncle, Aunt, Maude.

Enter, WHITE C.

White.   It is too late, they are making their way across
the lawn even now.

Enter, DEITRICH, C.

Mrs St Leon.   May heaven protect us!

Harry.   (*looking out of window*) Great heavens! White,
your house is one vast sheet of flames!

White.   It is indeed so.   Frank Duncan has one more
item scored against him.

Maude.   Harry, there is one avenue left; while they are
coming up the lawn, you escape through the cellar.

Harry.   Boys, at once to the cellar.   (*exit* R. 1 E.

Deitrich.   Boys come der cellar down. (*exeunt* L. 1 E.

Col St L.   Thank heaven they are safe!   (*crash*

Enter, FRANK DUNCAN, HARKER *and* GUERRILLAS, C.

Frank D.   Caged at last! (*looks around*) Gone!   Old
man, where is that sniveling Yankee nephew of yours?

Col St L.   Out of your reach, you infernal cut-throat!

Frank D.   'Tis false!   I will have him yet.   Search the
house from top to bottom.   Five hundred dollars for Harry
Pearson dead or alive!

(*exit* HARKER *and* GUERRILLAS, R. 1 E.

Col St L. He has escaped from your clutches, and is safe.

Frank D. Silence, old man! (*looking through window*) What is that I see? Harry Pearson making his way across the plantation towards the woods. (*discovers rifle*) Not so safe as you may think, he has left means for his own destruction. (*points rifle through window*

Maude. (*snatches revolver from his belt*) Fire that rifle at Harry Pearson and my hand will send a bullet through your heart! (*picture*) Now he has reached the woods and is safe. (*drops revolver*

Frank D. (*sneeringly*) You shall pay dearly for this at some future time. As I have missed one bird I will make doubly sure of the other. Come along my beauty and do not anger me by any vain resistance.

(*grasps* MAUDE *by the arm*

Col St L. (*raising cane*) Leave the house or I will chastise you for your insolence!

Frank D. (*picking up revolver*) Chastise me, will you? Take that for your insolence. *shoots*

SL. LEON *falls*—MRS. ST. LEON *and* MAUDE *kneel by him.*

Mrs St L. Villain! You have murdered my husband!

Maude. Wretch! What have you done?

Frank D. I have but commenced my scheme of vengeance.

Enter, HARKER *and* GUERRILLAS, C.

Har. Smith reports that Union cavalry is approaching by the east road.

Frank D. Then we must at once to our saddles; bear that old dotard to the yard. (*they carry* Ss LEON *out* C.) As for you, Miss Maude, make all your preparations to become my wife on my return. (*exit*, C.

Maude, Come, mother, this place is no longer safe for us.

Mrs St L. Oh, where shall I go? My husband murdered in cold blood and my nephew driven from home.

(*exit* L. 1 E.

SCENE VI—*Same as scene* I. *Lights down*—COL ST LEON *discovered on bank,* R.

Enter, MRS ST LEON L., *supported by* MAUD—*cross over to* R., *and kneel.*

Mrs St L. This cross is heavier than I can bear. All, all is dark to me. Colonel, husband, may our Father above receive thee!

Maude. Mother, mother!

Mrs St L. Forgive me my daughter, if, in grief for the dead, I forgot the living.

Ener, HARRY, L. 1 E.

Harry. Those terrible forebodings are still haunting my mind. I could not leave until I had again beheld my uncle, aunt and cousin. Why, who are those kneeling there? Tell me, who is that lying there?

Mrs St L. Your uncle, who has been murdered.

Harry. My uncle murdered!   (*kneels in group*

Enter, FRANK DUNCAN *and* HARKER, R. 1 E.

Frank D. Into the house, set fire to it in several places, then escape by the rear.

Exit L., HARKER *crosses cautiously from* R. *to* L.—*exit* L.

Harry. My forbodings are realized, uncle, dear uncle, murdered and I not here to protect you. Why are you both so calm? Why do you not weep rivers of tears? See those white locks dyed with the life current from his gaping wounds. Who did this terrible deed?

Mrs St L. Frank Duncan.

Harry. Frank Duncan's image came into my mind with my uncle's as if some terrible link connected them together. You see I am calm, tell me all.

Maude. After you had gained the wood, Frank Duncan enraged at your escape, rudely grasped my arm, and tried to drag me from the room; father, seizing his cane, sought to protect me, when Frank Duncan shot him down in cold blood and fled immediately, hotly pursued by the Union cavalry who heard the ing.

Harry. Gone! Escaped! and I not nigh to avenge the wrong. Oh, why were the thunderbolts of heaven silent when such a bloody deed was done?   (*fires pistol*

Enter, WHITE, L. 1 E.

Harry. Hold, White, ask no questions until I have told you all—a story that will make the blood curdle in your veins. There lies my uncle, murdered by that fiend in human shape, Frank Duncan. (*fire seen in house*) What is that, our house in flames? let us save what we can. (*as door is opened the flames burst out*) Too late, too late! Aunt, Maude, pray for us. (*draws revolver and kneels*) Our mission is revenge!

Tableau—Curtain.

ACT II.

SCENE I—Log house or kitchen in 4. Set door R. 2 E *Set fire place* L. 2 E. *Bed against flat* C. *Table and stools* L. *Lights down. Storm—thunder and lightning.*

DEITRICH *in bed, with leg bandaged—curtains closed.*

Deitrich. O,-o-o, ah! Ouf I don'd believe I ish gusht voked up! (*thunder and lightning*) Dunder-weather? Vere ish all der beobles vot ish here gone doo? Gracious, how it rains! (*thunder*) Chimminatti! Oh, mine leg! I wish dot rebel dot shoot me ouf mine leg derein vas gusht here, I bet me five dollars dot he got licked. (*gets out of bed*) Vells, dot fire has gone out, und dem vellers has gone out, und if mine leg don'd trouble me so much I vould gone out doo. (*thunder—sits down* L.) Jimmy-gingle-wax! Vot an awful veller dot Captain Harry vas, he gone among dem rebels vellers gusht der same vot he dond care vedder he vas kilt or not. I don'd know vot he vas mean by such gonduct like does. (*knock, heard* R. 1 E.) Hallo, somepodies vas at dot doors—why aint it over on dis sides, dot door vas always on der wrong sides. (*knock*) Holds on a half an honr, I ish coming. (*starts*) A mans died in a hurry once, but he was awful sorry afterwards. Who vas on der insides out?

Harry. (*outside*) It is me, Harry.

Deitrich. Ish dot so? (*opens door*) Vell, by golly Captain, you got mineself pack yet, aint it?

Enter HARRY, R.

Harry. 'Tis a terrible night out, where is White?

Deitrich. Vell I vas gusht a sleepen und I voke up he vas gone out. (*lightning*) Dot rains like der tuyval.

Harry. Fix up a little, Deitrich, I expect company.

HARRY *sits* L., *leans head on table*—DEITRICH *goes to bed and closes curtain.*

Deitrich. Dot ish all nate now, I puts everyting in its blaces. (*picks up blanket and throws it* L.) Everyting ish is in its blaces. (*crosses to* HARRY) Say, Captain, I don'd see how it vas you gone among dem rebel vellers so much you gets kilt gusht so sure as mine name vas Deitrich.

Harry. Revenge! (*strikes table—startles* DEITRICH

Deitrich. Ish dot so ! (*crosses quickly to* R.

Harry. The night Frank Duncan killed my uncle, and burned our house, I swore an oath of vengeance; as a spy I have gained access into the rebel lines; four of his band have fallen by my hand and he shall soon follow them. I expect some Union officers, to whom I shall impart information of importance.

Deitrich. Vell, you needn't git mat apout it, but vy don'd you git yourself a nice uniforms like dot ?

Harry. Here we live secluded, no one knows our intentions, except those I expect; should I wear a uniform of blue I could not gain admittance into their lines. (*knock* R.) Ah. that is the signal, open the door Detrich.

Deitrich. Ish dot der signal, dey petter knock der house down. It ish notting but some old loafers, you see me gif dem eer G. B. P. D. I. (*unfastens door—sits* L., *greasing shoes with a candle.*

Enter, GENERAL U. S. A., COLONEL FRANKLIN *and* OFFICERS, R.

Harry. Welcome, gentlemen, I am glad to see you.

General. We thank you for your greeting, but, who have I the pleasure of addressing?

Harry. Harry Pearson, known to your army as "The Avenger."

Gen. Harry Pearson! Can you be the son of my old class-mate at West Point, Col. Pearson, the hero of Vera Cruz, and nephew of Col. St. Leon!

Harry. The same.

Gen. Where is your uncle?

Harry. Dead, foully murdered, and that is why I, in place of joining your ranks, lead the roving life of a spy. But time is flying, General, here are some important dispatches I captured from one of the enemy's couriers. They will attack your camp early to-morrow morning in overwhelming numbers, intending to capture the pickets and take you by surprise.

Gen. Then we will be prepared to receive them. Many thanks till I can reward your valuable services better. Join our ranks and I will see that you receive a commission and it will be safer, as I understand there is a heavy reward offered for you, dead or alive.

Harry. General, do not try to tempt me from fulfilling my oath. I will willingly impart to you any information which I can obtain, but now I only live for revenge.

Gen. Gentlemen, let us at once to our camp. Pearson, whenever you may wish to see me, send word by the same messenger as before. Adieu.

Harry. (*opens door*) Adieu, General, you shall soon hear from me again. (*they exit—closes door*) 'Tis clearing up, the worse for my undertaking.

Deitrich. Dot Sheneral vas a fine fellers Captain. I vonder if I efer git dot shoes on. (*putting on shoe*

White. (*outside*) I say, Deitrich, open the door!

Harry. Ah! White! I will open the door for him.

Deitrich. Dot's righd, I ish pusy. (*puts on shoe*
(HARRY, *opens door*

Enter, WHITE *conducting* BURT, *who goes* C.

Harry. Who have you there, White? A Confederate officer, as I live. (DEITRICH *puts candle on box behind him*

White. He strayed a little too close to our retreat, so we captured him, and brought him in. We did not know but you could use him for some purpose.

Harry You were right, I need a Confederate uniform, and at once.

Burt. Sir, as an officer in the Southern army, and captured in uniform, I demand that you treat me as a prisoner of war and a gentleman.

Deitrich. Yaw, we dreats you dot vay. (*burns coat tail*

Harry. We shall treat you as a gentleman and a soldier, but it is necessary that I have your coat and hat for a few hours.

Burt.   I protest against your taking either, sir.

Harry.   Then we shall be obliged to take them by force much as I regret the necessity.

Deitrich.   Now you gusht dake mine advice. (*points to* HARRY)   Dot Captain Harry vas an awful veller when he gits mat, I tole you dot.

Burt.   Rather than submit to personal violence, I give them up under protest.   (*takes off coat and hat*

Harry.   Are you not the bearer of dispatches?

Burt.   I refuse to answer. (*looks quickly at right boot*

Harry.   I will trouble you to take off your right boot.

Deitrich.   (HARRY *holds* BURT) Captain, I dakes him off. (*takes hold of left leg*) Captain, dot veller vas right-handed in his left leg. (*pulls off right boot, falls over, and papers fall out of boot, gets up*) Of I don'd pelieve I broke sometings, by jibbity. (*business of rubbing himself*

Harry.   (*front, reading papers*) The very thing. With these papers I can make my way to headquarters. (*puts on* BURT'S *coat and hat, and whiskers from box on table*) I am going inside the Confederate lines.   Guard your prisoner well, as upon your vigilance depends my safety.

Deitrich.   I lets you out, Captain.   (*they exit*

White.   We will have to compel you to remain here until the Captain returns; so make yourself as comfortable as possible, only remember, the first effort you make to escape will be met by a closer confinement.

Enter, DEITRICH, R.

Deitrich.   Dot's so, der closer confined der petter you vas.   Look out vonce.   (*goes* L., *front*

Burt.   I will try and get a little sleep, if you can spare me a blanket.

White.   (*gets blanket*) There, make yourself at home. (*yawns*) I guess I am a little sleepy too.   Deitrich, (*goes to him*) Deitrich, you stand guard for a couple of hours, then I will relieve you.   Why, how sleepy I am. (*yawns*) Well, I'll turn in.

          (*takes blanket and lays down before fire* L., BURT, C.

Deitrich.   Sthand gart, dot's always der vay, I got to sthand gart all der dime. (*up stage*) Charley White is der

meanest man I efer saw, he makes me sthand gart. (*to* BURT)
Shut up yer left eye, I kick yer whole het off. (*takes gun,
pistol and sword, should be old, from under bed, lays sword
on table*) Dot's what I calls preparations for war. (*looks
at gun in right hand, then at pistol in left hand*) Dot's
der olt fader und dot's der leedle poy. Vhy, dot's a son ouf
a gun. Sthand gart! Anyting I likes ven I sthands gart
ish to dook a smoking. I dooks a smoking. (*examines box
then pockets*) Where ish mine bipes? (*looks in bed*) Aha,
I goes ter ped mit dot bipes. Now I dooks a smoking.
(*takes tobacco from box, light pipe with candle, burns nose*)
I don'd like dot. (*business of lighting pipe*) I kinder feels
dot sleepiness mineself. (*yawns*) I feels exactly as ef I—
(*looks at* BURT) I tought dot veller vas escaped, dot ain't
so—I gusht dook dot smoking den I stands gart.
(*business of getting pipe to mouth—commences to snore*

Burt. (*rises cautiously and goes to door*) Sleep on, my
Teutonic friend, your drowsiness has proved my salvation.
(*exit*

Deitrich. Scat! dem cats dey trouble me all der dime
ouf I don'd look out. I got ter sleepen'—hallo, mine bipe
has gone out! I gusht lights dot bipe, den I vaiks around
so I don'd gat to sleepin'. (*goes for the candle when he dis-
covers* BURT *is gone—drops pipe and looks around*) Oh,
Misder White, dot brisoner done escaped by himself out!
White. (*jumps up, grasps gun*) The prisoner gone!
How did he escape?
Deitrich. I gusht set down to dook a smoken und ven I
look around dot brisoner vas no vhere I see him.
White. Most likely you was asleep.
Deitrich. Nein, I vasn't asleep.
White. Come, Deitrich, we must re-capture that rebel,
or Harry is lost! (*exit* R.
Deitrich. (*putting on overcoat*) I got him pack again
so help me gimminy jinglewax (*exit with gun, pistol, sword*

SCENE II—*Landscape in 2.*

Enter, TEDDY L. 2 E., *on guard.*

Ted. I wish this tarnal war was ended. It is nothing
but foight aud stand on guard all the time. (*yawns*) I

haven't had a dacent night's rest for a week, and they have given us orders to be extramely watchful to-night. Halt, who comes there? (*looks* R.

Harry. (*outside*) A friend.

Ted. Advance and give the countersign.

Enter, HARRY R. 2 E.,

Harry. I have dispatches of the utmost importance and must see the General at once.

Ted. I will sind for the officer of the guard. (*looks* R.) Most likely this is the Gineral approaching, he sometimes comes around the outposts. Halt! who comes there?

Har. (*outside*) Grand Rounds.

Ted. Advance, Sergeant of Grand Rounds and give the countersign. (*enter* SERGEANT, *gives countersign.*) Countersign correct, pass rounds. (*exit to place. As Grand Rounds enters* L.. TEDDY *steps forward, salutes* HARKER) Officer of the guard, this officer here says he has despatches of importance for the Gineral. (*resumes station*

Gen. Well, sir, what papers have you?

Harry. (*producing papers*) General these dispatches were handed me by Major St. Clair, who has been severely wounded, and he requested me to deliver them to you in person.

Gen. Thanks, but to whom am I indebted for their safe delivery?

HARKER *who has been watching* HARRY, *draws revolver.*

Har. Do not attempt to escape.

Gen. What means this outrage, Lieutenant?

Har. (*pulling off* HARRY'S *whiskers*) General, allow me to introduce Harry Pearson, the Union Spy, more properly known as "The Avenger." (HARRY *folds his arms*

Gen. Ha! Then you are the man we are ordered to keep a close watch for. What infernal scheme have you on hand now that brings you into our lines?

Harry. I refuse to answer any questions.

Enter, FRANK DUNCAN, L. 1 E.

Frank D. General, I just heard of your intended surprise of the Union camp to morrow morning, and I come to volunteer the services of my band. What! Pearson. Ha, ha! my fine bird, caged at last.

Gen. You know him, Duncan, who is he?

Harry. The avenger of my uncle's murder!

(*grasps him by the throat*

Gen. Secure him, guards. (TEDDY *and* HARKER *seize him*) Young man, your case is desperate; I have orders to shoot you as soon as captured.

Harry. Such is generally the custom of Guerrillas, but hark you, General, it is life for life, a "Gray for a Blue."

Gen. I do not take your meaning.

Harry. But a few miles from here your courier is a prisoner. if I do not return my men will hang him to the first tree.

Enter, BURT R. 1 E.

Burt. General, I was captured by a party of scouts but a short distance from here, and—(*points to* HARRY) there stands their leader. I'll trouble you for my coat and hat.

Harry. Now my fate is sealed.

(*takes off coat and hat and hands them to him*

Gen. (*shakes hands with* BURT) Allow me to congratulate you. (*to* HARRY) And now to mete out to you the penalty prescribed by my superior.

Frank D. General, there is a little matter of long standing between the prisoner and myself, and if my well-known services would entitle me to the privilege of carrying out his sentence, you can call on me for any favor in return.

Gen. Your request shall be granted. Captain Duncan, you will see that my orders are strictly carried out, and these soldiers will be under your command until I receive your report. Come Lieutenant and Sergeant, let us at once to our quarters. (*exit* GENERAL *and staff* R. 2 E.

Frank D. Harry Pearson you are at last in my power. Prepare for the journey which you are about to take into a new country.

Harry. When I first undertook the hazardous life of a spy, I made all preparations to meet death face to face; but I warn you, Frank Duncan, by murdering me, you will not escape your just doom, for others are on your path who will execute the oath I swore against the murderer of my aged uncle.

Frank D. No more, I will hear no more. Teddy, place him yonder. (TEDDY *places* HARKER R. 2 E.) Now, men—ready—aim——

Shots heard R. *Exit* FRANK DUNCAN, TEDDY *and* GUERRILLAS, L. 2 E.

Enter, WHITE *and* DEITRICH, R. 2 E. WHITE *hands* HARRY *a gun.*

White. Take this gun; we must at once gain the protection of our cabin, or all will be taken.

Harry. Thanks, White, but let us start at once. That was a close shave for me. (*exit* R.

Deitrich. I fights mineself like der tuyval, aint it?

Looks around, seeing the rest have gone, exits hastily R.

Enter, FRANK DUNCAN *and* GUERRILLAS, L. 2 E.

Frank D. Escaped! Follow me at once in their path; take them dead or alive! (*exit* GUERRILLAS, R.

Enter, HARKER, BURT, GENERAL *and staff,* L. 2 E.

General, the spy has escaped, rescued by his friends who have killed our pickets.

Gen. Escaped! Have you ordered out an attachment in pursuit?

Frank D. Yes, General, at once.

Gen. Follow them yourself; leave not a stone unturned to effect his re capture; then take him, if alive, to Belle Isle —let him starve for his audacity. (*exit* FRANK DUNCAN, R.) Gentlemen, let us at once to the attack—all now depends upon quick action. To your saddles immediately—ride for your lives. One hour in the field, is worth a whole day here. (*exeunt* L. 2 E.

SCENE III— Wood in 1. Rain heard.

Enter, HARRY, WHITE *and* DEITRICH L., *quickly.*

Harry. At last we are free from those human bloodhounds.

White. Yes, we have thrown them off the scent; let us to our retreat, gather whatever we wish to take with us, and abandon this section for a time at least.

Harry. You are right, since Burt knows of its whereabouts, the place will be made too hot to hold us. Deitrich, you stand guard here, while we get ready for a start. Can you keep your eyes open now?

Deitrich. I can do dot, und if any rebels come ouf me I kills mineself ouf him, dot's so.

Harry. Come, White, let us hasten.　　　*(they exit* R.

Deitrich. (*crosses* R.) I must look ouf I got colt in my leg, I got der croup und den I die, und ouf I die I prings my barents pald heds do der graves mid sorrows. (*enter* TEDDY, L., *in haste*) Sthop quick! Who vas you?

Ted. Don't yese remimber me, Deitrich—Teddy O'Connor.

Deitrich. You vas der veller dot blay me ouf der drumps und shoots und der mit its hed do both ends down. I guess not.

Ted. Well, I am sorry for any misunderstandin' we hed, sure, an' I axes yere pardin.

Deitrich. You can't fool dis dutchman, nary dime—March! (*aims gun,* TEDDY *attempts to put hand in pocket*

Ted. Ye dirty spalpeen ye, but—

Deitrich. Shut up, no nonsense.

Enter, FRANK DUNCAN, L.

Deitrich. Sthop quick—trow up yer hants—mark dime ·--or I kilts mineslf.　　　　　*(they mark time*

Frank D. You infernal Dutchman, I'll—

Deitrich. No dalking mit der shentleman on guart.

Enter, BURT, L.

Deitrich. Sthop, quick—trow up yer hants—keep him oop, or I vires.

Enter, HARKER *and* GUERRILLAS, L.　HARKER *creeps cautiously towards* DEITRICH.

Deitrich. Ouf I vas a gommander ouf such a vellers like you, I vould start a graveyarts—vall in—

HARKER *pinions* DEITRICH'S *arms,* FRANK DUNCAN *places handkerchief over his mouth,* TEDDY *takes his gun, goes* L., *points gun at him.*

Ted. There, ye dirty spalpeen. Ye wouldn't shake hands wid Teddy O'Connor—

Frank D. Silence, fool! Do you want to alarm our game? Take him along with us.

(GUERRILLAS *pick up* DEITRICH

Har. Now, Captain, our game is once more within our reach.   (*exeunt* R.

SCENE IV— *Same as scene 1, Act II.*

Enter, GENERAL U. S. A., COLONEL FRANKLIN *and two* OFFICERS, R.

Gen. Pearson not here? what could have become of him?

Colonel Franklin. Most likely he has gone on one of his many expeditions, and will return ere long.

Gen. I fear for his safety. Since learning that he whom we knew so long as "The Avenger," was the son of my old friend, Colonel Pearson, I have taken a great interest in his welfare.

Col F. I hear footsteps, General; you are imperiling your safety by remaining so long outside our lines.

Gen. No man, who is an honorable soldier, whether general, or private, should be afraid to meet death in any form or shape.

Col F. The footsteps are approaching this way; let us sell our lives dearly if they are enemies. (*draws revolver*

Enter, HARRY *and* WHITE, R.

Gen. Ah! returned—I had fears for your safety.

Harry. This has been an eventful night to me, General. After you left here I returned to the Confederate camp in disguise, was discovered, and about to be shot, when my brave friends rescued me. Our retreat is known, and as Frank Duncan's guerrillas were in full chase after us, you had better leave at once, and I will shortly follow you.

Gen. Again you have placed me under obligations to you. To-morrow I wish you near me if there is a battle to be fought. Will you accept a position on my staff?

Harry. Yes, but for the day only. This is my place until I have fully avenged all wrongs. But, General, fly ere it be too late. (GENERAL, COL. FRANKLIN *and* OFFICERS, *exit* R. HARRY *throws himself on bed.*

Harry. Again those terrible forebodings of evil come before my mind. What do they foretell? Can they mean danger to my aunt and cousin? Oh, my poor unhappy South, why did you bring this righteous judgment upon you?

White. Come, Harry, we have not much time to lose. (*noise heard*) Hark! There is some one approaching.

(HARRY *jumps up and opens door—shot heard*

Harry. (*closing door*) That was a narrow escape. We will have to make a stand here, as it is too late for flight.

White. They must have either killed or captured Deitrich, though I did not hear a shot fired.

Har. (*outside*) Surrender and your lives will be spared, resist and we will burn the house.

Harry. (*shoots through window*) Take that for your answer. (*shots heard, then all is still*

White. What can they be doing?

Harry. They are gathering brush to fire the house. We must escape by the secret passage; you go while I keep them at bay. (*fire lighted*

White. 'Tis you they want, let me stay.

Harry. There is no time for argument, go at once.

WHITE *exits through trap. Door bursts open, enter* GUERRILLAS—HARRY *fires, one falls. Enter,* FRANK DUNCAN *and* HARKER, *who grasp* HARRY *as he enters trap.*

Frank D. Ah, my bird, caught again. This time you go to Belle Isle. (TEDDY *slips head first down trap*

Tableau—Curtain.

ACT III.

Here a Battle Scene may be introduced, when wanted, with Marches, Drills, Evolutions, &c.

ACT IV.

SCENE I—Same as Act 1, Scene 1.

UNCLE NED *and* NEGROES *discovered.*

Uncle Ned. Help de ole man on de bench, he wants to tole you something. (*they help him on bench*) Now, you

common niggahs, listen to what I tole yer; Missis says dat
yer are all free. (*all shout*) Dat yer ken go when yer
please, and whar yer please widout any Massa or Missus.
(*shout*) Massa Lincum dun sign de mancipashun proclama-
shun, so dat now yuse as good as white folks. (*shout*) So
all dose dat wants to work for demselves, pack up dere duds
and bid good-by to Missus.

             (*all exit* L , *but* UNCLE NFD *and* SAM

Sam. Uncle Ned, what is you gwine to do?

Uncle Ned. Sam, I was born on dis plantation, and
when Massa St. Leon was a little boy I toted him around,
and now dat he is dead and gone, does ye 'spose I'm gwine
to go away and leab de ole Missus?

Sam. Look a heah, Uncle Ned, you is as good as de
white folks; now why doesn't you join de Bobolishun party
and run for Congress?

Uncle Ned. You can do dat, Sam, as for me, I'll stick
to de ole plantation.

Sam. Well, good-by Uncle, dis chile is gwine, suah.

Uncle Ned. Good-by, Sam, and when yer gits to Congress don't forgit yer ole uncle. (*exit* SAM, L) 'Taint no
use talkin', dem darkies 'ull wish dey was back on de ole
plantation fore long.

      Enter, MRS. ST. LEON *and* MAUDE, L. 1 E.

Mrs St L. How well our old home has been made to
look.

Maude. Yes, mother, it was a miracle that naught but
the kitchens and upper chambers were distroyed.

Uncle Ned. (*bowing*) Beg pardon, Missus, but de ole
house looks kind of natural.

Mrs St L. Yes, Uncle, just as natural as of old; but did
you instruct the hands that they were now free to go where
they please?

Uncle Ned. Yes, Missus, and heah dey cum.

          (NEGROES *cross* L., *to* R., *with bundles*

Negroes. Good-by Missus—good-by Uncle Ned.

Mrs St L. Farewell—a kind farewell to all.

Maude. How sad one feels to even part from a servant.

Mrs St L. Good-bye, Uncle Ned, 'tis with the deepest
regret I part with you.

Uncle Ned. Missus, I isn't a gwine. I was born on dis plantation, and wid your leab I'll die heah. I'se ole now, Missus, and can't do much; but what I can do I will do. You won't send me away, Missus?

Mrs St L. No, Uncle Ned, while I have a roof over my head you shall share it with me.

Uncle Ned. Tank you, Missus, tank you; any place is good enough for me.

Maude. If Harry were only here to enjoy this, our return to the old homestead.

Mrs St L. I fear Maude, for his safety; 'tis over sx month since we have heard aught of him.

Enter, DEITRICH, R. U. E., *in haste.*

Deitrich. Dundervetter, vich vay I goes? Hallo, dot's Misdur Harry's folks. Ouf yer blease, dot pig repel veller vas afder me und I don'd know vich vay I gone.

Maude. Go into the house; there you will find some old clothes with which to disguise yourself.

Deitrich. Ish dot so.   (*exit* L.

Maude. Mother, we must detain his pursuers at all hazards. Uncle Ned, you run down the lawn, and throw them off the track if you can.

Uncle Ned. I'se gwine, Miss Maude, and if dey insist on cumin', I'll scrunch dem like a ped-pug.   (*exit* R. U. E.

Mrs St L. God grant we can save him from those terrible men.

Maude. If they belong to Frank Duncan's guerrillas, they are as bloodthirsty as their master.

Mrs St L. 'Tis strange that Frank has not troubled us since the fire.

Maude. He knows my feelings, and perhaps has foregone his determination to force me to become his wife.

Uncle Ned. (*outside*) I tell you, Massa Harker, dat dey haint nobody cum dis way, suah.

Har. (*outside*) Stand aside you black rascal—I'll see for myself.

Enter, HARKER, *two* GUERRILLAS, *and* UNCLE NED, R.

Har. Ah, ladies, excuse me.

Maude. John Harker, what means this outrage? I think that you and your villainous master have injured this family enough, without putting us to further trouble.

Mrs St L. Leave this plantation at once, or I will make a complaint to your superiors.

Har. (*bowing*) My superiors would pay but little attention to one that bears the reputation of being the aunt of a Union Spy. I am sorry to trouble you, Mrs. St. Leon, but a prisoner has escaped from us, and we have traced him here.

Mrs St L. I assure you that you will not find him inside of my house, but Mr. Harker, can you tell me any news of concerning my nephew, Harry.

Har. (*aside*) Here is an opportunity to throw in a word for Frank Duncan. (*aloud*) Yes, madam, six months ago Harry Pearson was captured by the Confederate forces, and condemned to be hung as a spy; through the intercession of Frank Duncan, he was reprieved, and is now in prison at Belle Isle.

Maude. Then Frank Duncan had some other of his villainous schemes in view. Perhaps he is being slowly starved to death, like so many of our poor boys.

Har. We are losing time in parleying thus. Men search the house. (HARKER *and* GUERRILLAS *start forward*

Maude. Hold! You enter that house at your peril! (*draws revolver—at* C.) If your master is rowdy enough to take advantage of two unprotected ladies, then I am woman enough to defy you all. (*picture*

Har. Stand aside, or I will order my men to fire.

Maude. Coward, do you fear one woman? You can enter the house, but you will not find a single soul within. (*aside*) 'Ere this he has escaped by the rear door.

Har. Search the house from top to bottom. (*they exit*) If he is found within, rest assured your conduct will be reported to our Commanding General.

Mrs St L. We will abide the issue.

Enter, DEITRICH, L. 1 E., *disguised as a woman*

Deitrich. Ouf yer blease, vas you der laties ouf dot houses?

Mrs St L. Yes, what can we do for you?

Deitrich. Hire me. (*aside*) I bin Deitrich.

(*crosses* L., HARKER R.

Maude. What can you do my good woman?

Deterich. I can vash, I can make peds, and I can vait on der laties.

Mrs St L. I think we shall need your services, as all of our help are gone.

Deitrich. All right, I hires you. Look ouf dot nice veller mit a gay uniforms, I vonder vedder my peau has got von like dot.

Har. Did any one pass you as you were coming across the plantation?

Deitrich. Who vas dot yer tole me.

Har. Did you see a man as you came along?

Detrich. A mans?

Har. Yes, a man.

Deitrich. Vas he dressed mit plue clothes, nnd a gap like dot vay?

Har. Yes, yes—

Deitrich. I don'd see somepodiy.

Har. Curse you for a stupid dutch fool. (*exit* L.

Deitrich. Gimminy, don'd I fools him. (*dances*

Maude. Be quiet, if he should suspect your trick, all is lost.

Deitrich. Here he cums.

Enter, HARKER *and* GUERRILLAS, *from house.*

Har. He is not in the house, come men, this way. (*exit* L.

Mrs St L. Thank heaven, he is gone.

Deitrich. Don'd I tink I vas a gone goose. Put don'd I makes a nice laties fer der situation? (*grecian bend to* L.

Maude. Hasten into the house—they may return.

Deitrich. I do dot, und ef you has no objections I dook dese clothings und I gone afder Misdur Harry.

Mrs St L. Do you think he can be freed, Deitrich?

Deitrich. I gits him free gusht as sure as mine name is Deitrich.

Mrs St L. Come into the house, there we can araange some means to send him relief. (*exeunt* L.

SCENE II—Landscape in 1.

Enter, WHITE, L.

White. I can gain no information of Harry's whereabouts. Twice have I been inside the Confederate lines, and returned disappointed. (*looks* R.) Who is that coming this way—a woman, as I live.

Enter, DEITRICH, R., *courtesies.*

Deitrich. Ouf yer blease, can yer told me der vay I gone to dot willages?

White. Yes, my good woman, but are you not afraid to be so near the rebel lines, and alone?

Deitrich. Nein, I bin afraids not, mine husband vas dot repel vellers.

White. Come along, I will show you the way.

Deitrich. Sharley White, I gusht been ashamet ouf yer.

White. What—Deitrich?

Deitrich. Yaw, und yer called me mine goot vomans—Sharley ef I didn't know dot vas yer, I should tink yer vas makin' love to me.

White. Why, I heard that you had been captured.

Deitrich. Yaw, I vas tooken brisoner by dem repel vellers, but I told 'em I knowed vhere you vas hiting, so dey dook me along to show der blace, und vhile dey was sleepen I valks off.

White. Well, I am glad to see you, but what means this disguise?

Deitrich. Misdur White, Harry is a brisoner at Pelle Isle, und py jiminny I gets him oud.

White. Harry a prisoner at Belle Isle—then I will disguise myself as an old man and go with you. Meet me near the ruins of our old cabin.   (*exit* R.)

Deitrich. I meets you all right, don'd been afraid of dot. Don'd I fools mineself mit Sharley? He says, "don'd been afraid my goot vomans." Afraid! Oh, I guess not. Now I must go right square and git Misdur Harry from dot brison out.

Enter, HARKER, L.

Har. Confound that Dutchman, how he fooled me. Ah, that dutch woman I saw at St. Leon's.

Deitrich. How you do, Misdur ?   (*courtesies*

Har. Do you know that I think you are not such a fool as you look ?

Deitrich. Ish dot so ?

Har. And come to look, you resemble that dutch prisoner I had this morning.

Deitrich. (*aside*) So mine gootness gracious, I's petter I got out ouf dis blaces.

Har. Yes, and I will have to search you before you leave here.

Deitrich. I gusht been ashamet ouf you to dalk dot **vay** to a boor vomans dot's all ouf herself in dis vide vorlt.

Har. Alone or not, I am determined to search you.

As HARKER *grasps his left hand,* DEITRICH *draws horse pistol and knocks him down.*

Deitrich. Dook dot, und don'd you nefer interfere mit **a** lone vomans dot's on der highvays. How you know put **I** vas Jeff Davis in betticoats ?   (*exit* R.

Har. (*rising*) Curse that infernal she devil, though I believe it was that Dutchman in disguise. How heavy my head feels ; I will find my men, then pursue and capture him.   (*staggers out* L.

SCENE III—Stockade or prison in 3. Lights half down.

HARRY, *and Union* PRISONERS, *discovered lying on stage* L. *Rebel* GUARD *on stockade. Tableau—"Prisoner's Dream of Home."*

Harry. Oh, God, will these inhuman fiends ever bring me anything to eat ? (*rising up*) For thirty-six hours not even a crumb has passed my lips. Can Frank Duncan mean to keep that fearful oath he swore when I was first incarcerated in this horrible den. Does he think he can starve me into acquiescence to his wishes ? Though naught but a ghastly skeleton were left of my once strong frame, I would still bid him defiance. The hope of once more seeing my poor aunt and cousin is all that sustains me now.

Enter, FRANK DUNCAN, R. 1 F., *with* GUARDS.

Frank D. Ah, good evening, Harry Pearson, your rations do not agree with you, if I should judge by your present condition.

Harry. Do you come here to mock my sufferings, inhuman fiend that you are?

Frank D. I come as a friend, to bring you this, my last offer.

Harry. Speak man. what would you say?

Frank D. I am in full command of this prison at the present time; here you are slowly but surely starving. Not many weeks will elapse ere you will sink into your grave, unknown and uncared for. I offer you life and liberty. Leave the Northern army—join us; tell Maude that you owe all to me, and rank and riches shall be yours. Refuse me and your tortures shall be tenfold.

Harry. I do refuse you, and with scorn. You offer me life and liberty, the two greatest boons to an American heart—but at what a price? My manhood. I warn you, Frank Duncan, should you fulfill your threat and kill me, my spirit would haunt you till your dying day, the same as my poor murdered uncle's does at the present.

Frank D. (*aside, looking around*) What can he mean? Does he too, see that old man, with gory locks and haggard face. Why do I conjure up such fancies. (*aloud*) Harry Pearson, beware how you refuse this, my last offer.

Harry. Though death stood ready to claim me instantly, my answer would remain the same.

Frank D. Then starve and rot here, you infernal Yankee spy; as for Maude, I will tear her from her home at once, and if she refuses to become my wife, I will make her beg at my feet for the position.

Harry. Inhuman fiend! but go—leave me.

Frank D. I leave you now, but remember that Frank Duncan always keeps his oath. (*exit* R)

Harry. Heaven is now my only hope—I will not repine, but try to say "Thy will, not mine, be done."

Prisoner. Will they ever bring us food?

Harry. Do not be down-hearted, comrade; when all earthly hope forsakes you, look to heaven for guidance.

Enter, FRANK DUNCAN, R. 1 E.

Frank D. Guards, be extremely vigilant; shoot the first

prisoner that crosses the dead-line. Thirty days furlough for a dead Yank.

Enter, DEITRICH *and* WHITE, R., *in disguise, followed by* GUARD, *with lantern.*

Frank D. Here are the prisoners; look around and see if you can find the one you are in search of.

Deitrich. Now Misdur officer, you tink I find miné boor huspant mit all dese brisoners?

Harry. (*aside*) Deitrich here—what can all this mean?

DEITRICH *gets between* WHITE *and* FRANK DUNCAN, WHITE *passes revolver to* HARRY.

Deitrich. Now Misdur officer, you go mit me und mine boor deaf und dumb vater tills ve finds him.

Frank D. Well, we will find him if he is here, and your request for his release shall be granted. (*exit* L.

Deitrich. (*speaks loud*) Cum ve vill find boor Deitrich.

(WHITE *nods his head, exit with* DEITRICH, L,

Harry. Hope again spring to my heart; with this weapon I can, at least, take life for life. (*lies down*

Enter, TEDDY, R. 2 E., *cautiously.*

Ted. Begorra, there goes that murtherin' spalpeen, Captain Frank Duncan, so that I'll have at laste a minit to look for Mister Harry Pearson.

Harry. Who speaks my name?

Ted. Phwist, ye divil! An' sure are yese Mistir Harry Pearson?

Harry. That is my name, but who are you?

Ted. Sure me name is Teddy O'Connor. Don't yese remimber the time that I came to your uncle's place, nothin' but a skeleton : an' sure didn't ye, like a big-hearted fellow as ye are, take me into the kitchen, an' give me plinty to ate and dhrink.

Harry. Are you the one?

Ted. Yis, an' fearin' yese might be hungry, sure I brot ye a loaf of bread.

Harry. (*takes bread*) Thank you, my brave fellow, and be assured that Teddy O'Connor will never be forgotten by me.

Ted.   Here's a ribil uniform for ye.   (*takes off coat and hat*)   The countersign is "Beauregard."   Bad luck to him, it ought to be Blackguard.

Harry.   "Cast thy bread upon the waters, for it will return ere many days."

Ted.   Throw it into the wather, is it?   Throw nice swate aitin' bread into the wather?   Begorra, I wouldn't gev it to ye if I thought ye was goin' to throw it in the wather.   I'd better make myself scarce, as here comes Frank Duncan.

Enter, FRANK DUNCAN, DEITRICH, WHITE *and* GUARD, L.

Frank D.   Then he is not here?

Deitrich.   Nein, mine boor huspand ve don'd can vind him.   (*weeps*

Frank D.   Dry your eyes my poor woman, you may be more fortunate at Libby Prison.

Deitrich.   I tries dot blaces und hopes dot you got dot rewarts fer helpin' a boor vomans.

Frank D.   I can never do too much for a loyal Southerner.   Come to my office and I will give you a pass that will take you any place inside our lines.

Deitrich.   Cum, vater, cum, ve got der basses. (*all exit* R.

Harry.   Here, comrades, I have a loaf of bread.

All come front C., HARRY *divides bread.   In going back one man steps over the dead-line,* GUARD *shoots him, the others drag him back.*

All.   Shame!   Shame!   (*all exit slowly* L., *but* HARRY

Harry.   Another martyr to liberty—but morning is approaching—I must hasten to leave this infamous den.
                                       (*puts on rebel coat and hat, exit* R.

Voice.   (*outside*)   Halt!   Who comes there?

Harry.   (*outside*)   A friend.

Voice.   Advance and give the countersign—Countersign correct.

Enter, FRANK DUNCAN L. 1 E., *with* GUARDS

Frank D.   Once more to gloat over the sufferings of Harry Pearson, then visit Maude, and force her to become my wife. (*looks around*)   Not here!   Why 'twas but a moment ago I saw him in this very place.   Come to think,

who was that Confederate soldier who passed us at the gate?
Curses on him—he has escaped! Sound the alarm at once!
Let loose the blood-hounds! hunt him to death. (*exeunt* R.

SCENE IV—*Landscape in 1.*

Enter, DEITRICH *and* WHITE, L.

Deitrich. Vell, py golly, Sharley, ve got out ouf dot places
mit vigs on, aind it. (*noise* L.

Harry. Yes; but what is that noise at the prison. Can
they suspect us?

Deitrich. I gusht hope not.

Enter, HARRY, L., *in haste.*

Harry. Ah, friends, I have just escaped from that infernal prison.

Deitrich. Den dey got you pack again, py jibbity.

White. Strike at once for the swamps, and we will try
to throw your pursuers from the trail. (*exit* HARRY, R.

Deitrich. Ouf der gits Misdur Harry pack again, I plack
mine dwo eyes yet.

Enter, FRANK DUNCAN, BURT *and* GUERRILLAS, L.

Frank D. Did you see a man dressed as a Confederate
soldier pass along this road?

Deitrich. Cans't you dicht sprecken. Nix-cum-arous
all der vhile mit der hioelwirken.

Frank D. I want none of your infernal dutch lingo, but
plain English.

Deitrich. Oh, you nix-for-stay. I don'd seen any podies.

Frank D. Come on, men, at once for the blood-hounds,
they will find his trail. (*they exit* R.

Deitrich. Vell, Sharley, ve got rid ouf dem und you gan
dake off dem vig und viskers. Ven you had dose vite vigs
und viskers on, I tinks you vas mine grandfaders—now I
tinks you vas mine grandmudders. How you likes mine
dress? (WHITE, *takes off disguise*

White. Very well, Deitrich, but you are not in style.

Deitrich. Vhat is der reasons I aint in der styles.

White. Why you haven't any pin-back.

Deitrich. I makes a pin-pack. (*pins apron back*) How you likes me dot vay, put let's go und see if Frank Duncan catches Misdur Harry.

White. (*takes his arm*) Come along, hurry up. (*exit* R.

SCENE V—Rocky pass in 4. Set log R. *Set rocks* R. **3 E.**

Enter, HARRY, L. 1 E.—*falls.*

Harry. Hark! I hear the baying of those terrible blood-hounds—'tis too late for further flight. There are seven charges in this revolver—six for them and one for myself before I will be re-taken. (*fires* L.) One less. (*fires*) Missed! (*fires*) Both dead, and four charges left—these I will reserve for human blood-hounds. Now for the stream.   (*exit* R. 1 E.

Enter, FRANK DUNCAN, BURT *and* GUARDS, L. 1 E. HARRY *appears on log,* R.

Frank D. Just in time—die—

HARRY *fires—one* GUARD *falls.* FRANK DUNCAN *fires—* HARRY *reels.*

Harry. Oh, heaven! I'm shot. Frank Duncan, may my curse haunt you—   (*falls into stream*

Frank D. Let us leave this place. That curse will ring in my ears forever.   (*exit* L., *in haste*

Enter, DEITRICH, R., *who draws* HARRY *from stream.*

Deitrich. Ish dot so!

Tableau—Curtain.

ACT V.

SCENE I—Dark Wood or Rocky Pass in 4. Set trees and rocks R. *and* L. *Set fire* U. C.

BURT, TEDDY *and* GUERRILLAS, *discovered drinking.*

Burt. Fill up, boys, I've got a toast to offer. Here's to the Captain, although he wasn't with us when we captured this brandy from that old fool of a Dutchman, but, for all that, he's a trump in a fight. Come, boys, drink this standing. (*rise and drink*

Ted. No, the Captain wasn't along, but he had a smashing excuse. He was after a petticoat, one Maude St. Leon, and she is now imprisoned in the cabin beyant. (*points* L.

Burt. Well, if the Captain wants to run away with young and pretty females, spend his time billing and cooing, and leaving the lush to us, why—who cares? Not I, for one. Harry Pearson's death left the coast clear for him.

Ted An' sure it's meself doesn't think he's dead at all.

Burt. Didn't I see him fall into the stream after the Captain shot him?

Ted. Sure an' he'll be turning up some day like a cat wid nine lives.

Enter, FRANK DUNCAN, R.

Burt. Harry Pearson will never trouble us again.

Frank D. Who says he will? Whoever dared to make that assertion, lied. Fools, did I not shoot him down from the log, and watch him plunge headlong into the stream? Does not his curse ring in my ears—and when I try to sleep, do I not see him and his cursed uncle in my dreams? But no more—let me hear no more of him. I tell you once for all, he is dead—dead I say!

Burt. For heaven's sake never mention the subject again in his presence.

Frank D. Give me some brandy. (TEDDY *fills glasses*) Fill it up. (*lays hand on breast*) There is something here 'twould take oceans of liquor to remove.

Ted. (*aside*) Begorra, the double murder sits hard upon his conscience.

Enter, HARKER, R.

Frank D. What now, Harker?

Har. A wagon train is approaching by the turnpike, and our scouts report that it is weakly guarded.

Frank D. Men, at once to your saddles, leave not one Northern hireling to tell the tale. (*exit*, TEDDY, *and* GUERRILLAS, R.) Harker, conduct Maude St. Leon to this place, I wish a short conversation with her. (*exit* HARKER, L.) Now Maude St. Leon, you are in my power; I swore I would possess you, and I have kept my word. Harry Pearson is dead, and I have naught to fear from any source.

Enter, HARKER *and* MAUDE L.

Thanks, Harker, at once to the men and I will join you in a moment. (*exit* HARKER R. 1 E.) Hark you, girl; time enough has elapsed since the death of your cousin for all purposes of mourning; I am going on a short expedition and you must make preparations at once, as our marriage will take place to-night.

Maude. Frank Duncan, I am a prisoner, torn from a loving mother's arms. You murdered my father and cousin, and as you fear heaven's wrath do not carry your threat into execution.

Frank D. Good, I like to see a little spirit in the one I love. First, one kiss, and then to horse. (*goes toward her*

Maude. Back! I warn you not to approach.

Enter, HARKER R., *quickly.*

Har. The men are getting impatient, Captain.

Frank D. To horse at once. (*exit* HARKER, R.) I will postpone my chaste salute 'till my return. (*calls*) Teddy! Where can that Irishman be. Teddy!

Enter, TEDDY, R.

Ted. Here I am, sur.

Frank D. Keep a strict guard on that girl. I will hold you responsible for her safe keeping.   (*exit* R.

Ted. Begorra, look at the foine girl I've got to guard.   (*marches* R. *and* L.

Maude. He has gone at last! who will aid me now?

Ted. Begorra, Miss, its meself will do that same thing.

Maude. You? Why you belong to his band.

Ted. Yis, an' no, mam. It was meself that helped your lover Harry to escape from prison.

Maude. Only to be murdered in cold blood.

Ted. Don't belave it, Miss. Though I can't explain, I have rasons for sayin' I don't belave he was killed at all.

Maude. But what reasons have you for assisting me; do you not know that if you are discovered you will pay the penalty with your life?

Ted. I am aware of all that, but whin I was starvin', Harry Pearson gave me mate an' drink, an' Miss, Teddy O'Connor niver forgits a kindness.

Maude. Heaven will bless you, my friend; but is there no way to escape from here?

Ted. Not at present, the place is strongly guarded; but I will hasten to the Union camp an' return wid a large force.

Maude. Go at once. But first, have you a revolver?

Ted. Yis, take this, (*takes bottle from pocket*) excuse me, Miss, that was me spectacle case. (*hands her revolver*) Take this.

Maude. Warn the Federal General, who is an old friend of father's, of my danger.

Ted. Begorra, Miss, I'm the bye to do it. (*exit* R.

Maude. This shall be my protection if he fails to return in time. (*sits on rock* L.

SCENE II—*Wood in 2.*

Enter, GENERAL U. S. A., COLONEL *and* FRANKLIN R. 2 E.

Gen. 'Tis strange that nothing reliable has been reported by our many scouts concerning the fate of Pearson.

Col F. What do you think of the reprot that he was killed by Frank Duncan?

Gen. I hardly give it the least credence. (*looks* R.) Here comes White, whom I sent to obtain information concerning the whereabouts of Frank Duncan's band of Guerrillas.

Enter, WHITE, L.

Gen. What brings you back so quickly?

White. General, I had hardly set forth upon the expedition you sent me when I met one of Frank Duncan's men, who said he had information of importance to impart to you.

Gen. Where is this man?

White. But a short distance from here. I will call him. (*calls*) Teddy, Teddy O'Connor!

Gen. A more villainous set than those Guerrillas, never drew breath. Let me gain but a clue to their whereabouts, and they shall be blotted from the earth's surface.

Enter, TEDDY, L.

Ted. That's me name, an' how are yese, gintlemin?

White. This is the man, General.

Gen. Well, sir, what do you know concerning Frank Duncan's band?

Ted. Sure yer honor, they are encamped down on an old plantation about tin miles beyant this place. I left but a short time ago to git help to rescue a poor female woman from his clutches.

Gen. How many men compose his band?

Ted. Sure sur, ave I was on me oath, I should say about wan hundred, sur.

Gen. Who is this girl or woman that is imprisoned there?

Ted. Her name is Maude St Leon, sur.

Gen. The daughter of my old friend! Can you lead us to this plantation?

Ted. I'm the bye that can do that same thing, sur.

Gen. Do you know anything concerning Harry Pearson?

Ted. Sure, sur, didn't I help him to escape from Belle Isle prison.

Gen. You did, and where is he now?

Enter, HARRY, L., *with head bandaged.*

Harry. Here, General, once more ready to fight against any traitor to the glorious old Stars and Stripes.

Gen. (*shaking hands*) You are just in time, we were about making up a detachment to attack Frank Duncan's Guerrillas, and rescue your cousin Maude, who is held a close prisoner. But how did you escape?

Harry. 'Twill take but a few words to tell my story. I was imprisoned at Belle Isle for six months and nearly starved to death, when this friend (*points to* TEDDY) furnished me with a disguise and the countersign.

Ted. Sure that's me.

Harry. While in the swamps I was pursued by bloodhounds. I killed them both, and had gained a log which led across a stream, when I was discovered by Frank Duncan, who fired, the ball striking my head; stunned and faint from the loss of blood I fell into the water, but was rescued by Deitrich. I bade him mention to no one my rescue, wishing Frank Duncan to believe me dead. But let us start at once, I yearn for the moment when I can meet him face to face.

Enter, DEITRICH, R. 1 E.

Deitrich. Ah, Mr. Sheneral, I gusht cum down. What, Captain Harry, I tought I you vas in pet.

Harry. I was a short time ago, and would be yet if I had obeyed your orders. But Deitrich, we are making up a party to attack Frank Duncan's guerrillas.

Deitrich. Ish dot so. But Captain I don'd tink dot you vas lookin' vell enough for dot fightin' business.

Harry. I am good for many encounters with the enemies of my country.

Deitrich. Dot's me too.

Gen. Colonel Franklin, order your men to their saddles, and I will take command in person.

(*all exit* R., *but* DEITRICH, *and* TEDDY, *who crosses* L.

Deitrich. Vell, halio, Teddy!

Ted. Begorra, how are yese, Deitrick?

Deitrich. Shook. (*shake hands*) Vat vas you, a Union mans?

Ted. Well, I am.

Deitrich. Shook again, vas you sure you vas a goot Union mans? (*shake*

Ted. Sure I'm as good a wan as yese.

Deitrich. Took anoder shook. (*shake*) Vell, Teddy, ve got trough mit dot fighting business, I told you what ve vill do—ve go und take someting. Vill you took someting?

Ted. I'm the bye that will do that samc thing.

Deitrich. Let's took a valk. (*exeunt* R.

SCENE III—Same as scene 1. Lights partly down.

MAUDE, *discovered.*

Maude. Teddy not returned. I fear he has failed in his mission, if so, then my only resource will be this revolver he so kindly gave me. Hark, I hear Frank Duncan and his men returning. I had hoped for a longer respite from his presence.

Enter, FRANK DUNCAN, *and* MRS. ST. LEON, R. 1 E.

Frank D. I have brought you a visitor, Miss Maude.

Mrs St L. My dear, dear daughter! (*embracing her*

Maude. Mother!

Frank D. You can now retire to yonder cabin and make all arrangements for our approaching marriage, which takes place to-night.

Maude. Come mother, let us be together while we can.

(exit L.

Frank D. Everything is working to my wishes; by jove though, that was a fat haul to-day.

Enter, BURT, *and* GUERRILLAS, R., *with bottles.*

Well, boys, as you have done a good day's work, fill up your glasses and make a merry night of it.   *(fill glasses*

Burt. Here's a health, Captain, and many returns.

Frank D. Thank you, my brave men, and in return I will invite you to my wedding.

Burt. Long live the Captain. *(they cheer)* When does it take place, Captain?

Frank D. This night, in one hour. Fill up men and drink a bumper to my fair bride, Maude St. Leon. *(all drink*

Enter, HARKER, R.

Har. Captain, a large force of Union Cavalry is approaching by the main road; 'tis too late to retreat, we must meet them here.

Frank D. Out men, fall in and fight for your lives. *(exit* BURT *and* GUERRILLAS, R) Harker, where is that Irishman, Teddy?

Har. I have not seen him since morning.

Frank D. Curse him! 'tis he that has brought this Yankee horde upon us. At once to the men, have them ready to repel any attack that may be made.   *(exit* HARKER R.

Enter, MRS. ST. LEON, *and* MAUDE, L.

Mrs St L. The avengers are on your path, do not court destruction, fly, or your blood, will be upon your own head.

Frank D. What! Frank Duncan, who fears neither man nor devil, desert his men, what can you mean?

Maude. Do you not fear death, with such a terrible load of guilt upon your soul?

Frank D. I have no time to bandy words with women. Do not leave this place under any consideration.

(exit R., *in haste—shots heard*

Maude. Mother, I am sure my hour of deliverance has come.

Mrs St L. We will hope for the best. (*firing heard*

Enter, HARKER, R., *staggers to* C., *falls.*

Har. Mrs. St. Leon, I am dying—forgive me for all the pain and suffering I have caused you and yours—forgive—
(*dies*

Mrs St L. May God forgive you as freely as I do.

Maude. Oh, mother, I hope the Union army will be victorious.

Enter, FRANK DUNCAN, R.

Frank D. All is lost, but, Maude St. Leon, you shall be mine in death if not in life. (*draws dagger, starts toward* MAUDE—*shot heard*—*he staggers*) I'm shot, but death shall still wed us.

Enter, DEITRICH, R., *with gun, strikes* FRANK DUNCAN *who falls.*

Deitrich. How you like dot, Misdur Guerrillas?

Enter, HARRY, WHITE, GENERAL U. S. A., COL. FRANKLIN, OFFICERS *and* TEDDY, R.

Maude. Harry, are you alive and safe?

Harry. Yes, my dear Maude. Aunt, have you no word for me ?

Mrs St L. We welcome you as from the grave.

Frank D. (*rising slowly*) Curse you, Harry Pearson, can you not stay in your grave; and you, old man, go back from whence you came; do not stare at me with those glassy eyes. Back—back I— (*falls back dead*

Deitrich. I done dot. (*exit* L.

Maude. Misguided man, he is dead; and Harry, I am thankful that you did not stain your hands with his blood.

Harry. Let us try to forgive him for his many injuries to all. He is dead, and "The Avenger's" mission is ended.

POSITION OF CHARACTERS IN LAST TABLEAU.

GEN U. S. A.   COL. FRANKLIN.   WHITE.   TEDDY.

MAUDE.   HARRY.   MRS. ST. LEON.

DUNCAN.   HARKER.

CURTAIN.